REBECCA OF SUNNYBROOK FARM

KATE DOUGLAS WIGGIN

CONDENSED AND ADAPTED BY
LOUISE COLLN

ILLUSTRATED BY
RUTH PALMER

Dalmatian Press

The Dalmatian Press Children's Classics Collection
has been adapted and illustrated with care and thought,
to introduce you to a world of famous authors, characters, ideas,
and great stories that have been loved for generations.

Editor — Kathryn Knight
Creative Director — Gina Rhodes
And the entire classics project team of Dalmatian Press

ALL ART AND ADAPTED TEXT © DALMATIAN PRESS, LLC

ISBN: 1-57759-539-4 mass
1-57759-563-7 base

First Published in the United States in 2003 by Dalmatian Press, LLC, USA

Copyright © 2003 Dalmatian Press, LLC

Printed and bound in the U.S.A.

The DALMATIAN PRESS name and logo are
trademarks of Dalmatian Press, LLC, Franklin, Tennessee 37067.

11392

03 04 05 06 07 LBM 10 9 8 7 6 5 4 3 2 1

A note to the reader—

A classic story rests in your hands. The characters are famous. The tale is timeless.

This Dalmatian Press Children's Classic has been carefully condensed and adapted from the original version (which you really *must* read when you're ready for every detail). We kept the well-known phrases for you. We kept the author's style. And we kept the important imagery and heart of the tale.

Literature is terrific fun! It encourages you to think. It helps you dream. It is full of heroes and villains, suspense and humor, adventure and wonder, and new ideas. It introduces you to writers who reach out across time to say: "Do you want to hear a story I wrote?"

Curl up and enjoy.

DALMATIAN PRESS
ILLUSTRATED CLASSICS

ALICE'S ADVENTURES IN WONDERLAND

ANNE OF GREEN GABLES

BLACK BEAUTY

THE CALL OF THE WILD

DOCTOR DOLITTLE

FRANKENSTEIN

DR. JEKYLL AND MR. HYDE

HEIDI

HUCKLEBERRY FINN

THE LEGEND OF SLEEPY HOLLOW
RIP VAN WINKLE
THE SPECTRE BRIDEGROOM

A LITTLE PRINCESS

LITTLE WOMEN

MOBY DICK

OLIVER TWIST

PETER PAN

PINOCCHIO

POLLYANNA

REBECCA OF SUNNYBROOK FARM

THE SECRET GARDEN

THROUGH THE LOOKING GLASS

THE TIME MACHINE

TOM SAWYER

TREASURE ISLAND

WHITE FANG

THE WIND IN THE WILLOWS

THE WONDERFUL WIZARD OF OZ

CONTENTS

REBECCA ROWENA RANDALL — a young girl who lives with her aunts so she can go to school and help her family

LORENZO DE MEDICI RANDALL — Rebecca's happy, talented father who died when Rebecca was young

AURELIA SAWYER RANDALL — Rebecca's hardworking mother with seven children

HANNAH — Rebecca's sensible, patient older sister, who marries Will Melville

JOHN, JENNY, MARK, FANNY, AND MIRA — the younger brothers and sisters that Hannah and Rebecca help to raise

THE COBBS — the stagecoach driver and his wife ("Uncle Jerry and Aunt Sarah") who always have time for Rebecca

AUNT MIRANDA SAWYER — Rebecca's strict aunt – set in her ways, very neat and clean

AUNT JANE SAWYER — Rebecca's kind aunt, who helps Rebecca find ways to get along with Aunt Miranda

EMMA JANE PERKINS — Rebecca's most loyal and best friend

THE SIMPSON FAMILY — a large family in Riverboro, going through hard times

MISS DEARBORN — the teacher at the Riverboro school

ADAM LADD — the young gentleman who is "Mr. Aladdin" to Rebecca

REV. BURCH — a missionary who stays with his family overnight at the "brick house"

HULDAH MESERVE — a stylish fellow student at Wareham Academy

MISS MAXWELL — the teacher at Wareham Academy, who helps Rebecca to travel and write

REBECCA OF SUNNYBROOK FARM

CHAPTER ONE

Rebecca Randall

The old stagecoach was rumbling along the dusty Maine road. The day was warm, though it was the middle of May. Mr. Jeremiah Cobb had driven this mail route from Maplewood to Riverboro many times. He settled back with his hat pulled low.

There was only one passenger in the coach. It was a small dark-haired person in a tan dress. She, too, was trying to settle into the ride. But she was so slender and her dress was so starched that she kept sliding on the leather cushions. She tried to brace herself with her small, gloved hands. But whenever the wheels sank down into a rut,

or jolted over a stone, she bounced up into the air and down again. Each time, she pushed back her funny straw hat and tried to get settled again. Every now and then, she picked up her small pink parasol and bouquet of lilacs—or she peeked into a little bead purse. Mr. Cobb did not even know that his passenger was having such a bouncy, slippery ride.

A woman at the Maplewood station had asked Mr. Cobb to drive her little girl to Riverboro. The mother helped the child into the stagecoach, loaded a trunk, and then paid Mr. Cobb.

"Do you know Miranda and Jane Sawyer?" she asked. "They live in the brick house in Riverboro."

"Lord bless your soul!" replied Mr. Cobb. "I know 'em well!"

"Well, they are my sisters. I am Aurelia Randall, and this is my daughter, Rebecca. She is going to stay with them. They know she's coming. Will you keep an eye on her, please? You see, she's kind of excited… We've had a long trip. Yesterday we came on the train from the town of Temperance. We slept at my Cousin Ann's house, and then drove her buggy here—eight miles it is—all this morning. Well, good-bye, Rebecca.

Try not to get into any mischief. And sit quiet, so you'll look neat and nice when you get there. Don't be any trouble to Mr. Cobb."

"Good-bye, Mother. And don't worry. After all, I *have* traveled before."

The woman chuckled. "She's been to Wareham and stayed overnight. That isn't much traveling!"

"It *was traveling*, Mother," said the child eagerly. "It was leaving the farm, and packing a lunch basket, and riding in a buggy, and then on a train. And we carried our nightgowns!"

"Rebecca!" said the mother. "Haven't I told you before that you shouldn't talk of nightgowns and stockings and—things like that?"

"I know, Mother, I know. I just meant—"

Mr. Cobb slapped the reins, and the horses started on down the road.

"—I just meant—it really *is* traveling when—" Rebecca put her head out the window and yelled back to her mother, "when you carry a nightgown!"

Mrs. Randall watched the stagecoach rumble down the road in a cloud of dust.

"Mirandy will have her hands full, I guess," she said to herself. "But I think my sisters will be the making of Rebecca."

All this had been half an hour ago, and Mr. Cobb had forgotten about his passenger. Then, suddenly, he heard a small voice above the noise of the wheels. At first he thought it was a cricket, a tree toad, or a bird. He turned his head over his shoulder and saw a small shape hanging out of the window. It was the child! Her long black braid of hair was flying in the air. With one hand she held her hat. With the other, she was trying to poke at him with her pink parasol.

"Please let me speak!" she called.

Mr. Cobb pulled lightly on the reins to slow up the horses.

"Does it cost any more to ride up there with you?" she asked. "It's so slippery that I'm sliding around here. I'm almost black and blue. And the windows are so small, I can't see much outside."

"You can come up if you want to," Mr. Cobb said cheerfully. "There's no extra charge." He stopped the horses and helped her up to the seat beside him.

"Oh! This is better! I am a real passenger now! It's a good day, isn't it?" said the girl.

"Too hot, mostly. Why don't you put up your little parasol?"

"Oh dear, no!" she said. "I never put it up when the sun shines. Pink fades awfully, you know. I only carry it to church on Sundays—if it's cloudy. It's the dearest thing in life to me. Did you notice the double ruffle and ivory handle?"

Mr. Cobb took his first good look at the passenger perched by his side. The girl stared back with friendly curiosity. She looked to be about ten or eleven, but she seemed small for her age. Her plain little face was brown and thin. There was nothing unusual, really, about her— but those eyes! They lit up her face and glowed like two stars. They made him think of a verse from the Bible about faith—*the substance of things hoped for, the evidence of things not seen.* They almost seemed to look right through him to something deeper. "Why, those eyes," Mr. Cobb later told his wife, "could knock a person galley-west!"

"The ivory handle has scratches, you see," Rebecca went on. "That's because Fanny chewed it in church when I wasn't looking."

"Is Fanny your sister?"

"She's one of them."

"How many are there of you?"

"Seven. There's poetry written about seven children—*Quick was the little Maid's reply, O master, we are seven!* Mr. Wordsworth wrote it. He was a poet. He lived in England. I learned those lines in school. Hannah is the oldest, I come next, then John, then Jenny, then Mark, then Fanny, then Mira. Mira is named after Aunt Miranda. We're all named after someone. My name is taken out of the book *Ivanhoe*. My father knew all the best books, you see. His name was Lorenzo— Lorenzo de Medici Randall. Isn't that a fine name? Mother says we must always stand up for Father, because it was only bad luck that made us poor. Mira was born the day Father died. She's three now, and Mother says we're stopping at seven. We'll all have a lovely time when we're all grown up and the farm mortgage is paid off."

Mr. Cobb smiled. "Maybe we'd best share our names since we're goin' to be ridin' together. I'm Jeremiah Cobb, but most folks call me Jerry."

"My name is Rebecca Rowena Randall. I'm going to live with my Aunt Miranda and Aunt Jane Sawyer in the brick house in Riverboro."

"I know them well," replied Jerry. "Your farm back home ain't the old Hobbs place, is it?"

"No, it's just Randall's Farm. At least that's what Mother calls it. I call it Sunnybrook Farm. It matters what you name a place, don't you think? It has a chattering little brook with a white sandy bottom and lots of shiny pebbles. Whenever there's a bit of sunshine the brook catches it. It's always full of sparkles the livelong day."

Mr. Cobb began to realize what an unusual little person Rebecca was. "I guess you're in school and it ain't no trouble for you to learn your lessons, is it?"

"Not much. The trouble is to get the shoes to *go* to school. I've read lots of books, though. Any I can get! Have you read *Cinderella*, or *The Yellow Dwarf*, or *The Enchanted Frog*, or *The Fair One with Golden Locks*? I even try the hard ones like *David Copperfield*! I'll be going to school when I'm living with Aunt Miranda. And in two years I'm going to the Academy at Wareham. Mother says it ought to be the making of me!"

CHAPTER TWO

The Brick House

" 'Tain't far, now," Mr. Cobb told Rebecca when he saw the village of Riverboro in the distance. "I live 'bout half a mile beyond the brick house myself. You come see me—and ride with me while I deliver papers. Now you watch me heave this newspaper right onto Miss Brown's doorstep."

Mr. Cobb flung a packet and *pfft!* it landed on the front mat.

"Oh, how splendid!" cried Rebecca. "Just like the knife thrower Mark saw at the circus."

"Well, if your Aunt Mirandy will let you, I'll take you down to Milltown some day this summer when the stagecoach ain't full."

Rebecca was thrilled from her new shoes up— up to the straw hat and down the black braid. "Oh, to think I could see Milltown!" she whispered. But then her face changed. "I didn't think I was going to be afraid," she said quietly, "but I guess I am, just a little, when you say it's coming so near. Aunt Miranda wanted Hannah to come instead of me, but mother couldn't spare her. Hannah takes hold of housework better than I do."

"Would you go back?" asked Mr. Cobb.

She flashed him a brave look. "I'd *never* go back! I might be afraid, but I'd be ashamed to run. But I do think I better get back into the stagecoach. That's where Mother put me, and that's where a lady should sit. Would you please stop a minute, Mr. Cobb, and let me change?"

Mr. Cobb smiled and stopped the horses. He lifted the excited little girl down, helped her in, and put the lilacs and pink parasol beside her.

"We've had a great trip," he said, "and we've gotten to be friends, haven't we? You won't forget about Milltown?"

"Never!" she exclaimed. "And you're sure you won't, either?"

"Never! Cross my heart!" vowed Mr. Cobb.

The stagecoach rumbled down the village street between the green maples. Anyone who looked from their windows would have seen a little elf in a faded brown dress clutching a great bouquet in one hand and a pink parasol in the other. And anyone who could look closely might have seen two pale cheeks, and a mist of tears swimming in two dark eyes.

Rebecca's journey had ended.

"There's the stage turning into the Sawyer girls' yard," said Mrs. Perkins to her husband. "That must be the niece from up Temperance way. She'll be good company for our Emma Jane. Why, she looks dark as an Indian! Must be her Spanish blood. They used to say that one of the Randalls married a Spanish woman. Well, I don't know as that Spanish blood didn't give her somethin' special—she looks like an up-and-comin' child."

The stage came to the side door of the brick house. There stood two proper ladies—Aunt Miranda and Aunt Jane. Rebecca got out carefully. She put the bunch of faded flowers in her Aunt Miranda's hand.

Aunt Miranda greeted her stiffly. "You needn't have bothered to bring flowers. The garden's always full of 'em here when it comes time."

Aunt Jane kissed Rebecca. "Put the trunk in the entry, Jeremiah, and we'll get it carried upstairs this afternoon," she said.

"Well, g'bye, Rebecca," said Mr. Cobb. "Good day, Mirandy 'n' Jane. You've got a lively little girl there. I guess she'll be first-rate company."

Miss Miranda shuddered. "We're not much used to noise, Jane and me," she remarked.

They had been called the Sawyer girls when Miranda, Jane, and Aurelia were teenagers in the village. Miranda and Jane, spinsters of fifty and sixty, were still called the Sawyer girls. Miranda Sawyer was thrifty, hardworking, and very cold of heart. Jane was softer and gentler. It was Jane who had gone to nurse wounded soldiers in the War Between the States—after her fiancé had died in battle. She had not left Riverboro since.

Aurelia, Rebecca's mother, was the only one who had married. It was a "romantic marriage," she said. "A mighty poor one," her sisters said. Aurelia had a modest share of the Sawyer money. But Rebecca's father had lost it long before they bought the rundown Sunnybrook Farm. The handsome Lorenzo de Medici Randall was not gifted with making money. Farming was not in his soul. Instead, he taught weekly singing school, played violin, and "called off" at village dances.

Rebecca, of all the Randall children, was most like her father. She had his zest for life and music and his sense of humor. She sang alto by ear, danced without being taught, played the church organ. And she loved books, especially classics.

She was a thing of fire and spirit—a plucky girl. And she could be headstrong. She was not as patient as her older sister, Hannah. And not as steady as John. Aurelia thought she was too skittish and dreamy—and not responsible. Like her sisters, Miranda and Jane, Aurelia admired plain, everyday common sense. Rebecca did not seem to have much of this. And so Miranda and Jane were not looking forward to Rebecca's arrival—especially Miranda.

It had been several years since Miranda and Jane Sawyer had visited Sunnybrook Farm. They remembered Rebecca as wild, and Hannah as a quiet, dependable child. That is the reason her aunts had invited Hannah to Riverboro to live with them. The Riverboro schools would be better for her education. So, when they got their sister's letter saying she was sending Rebecca, they were shocked. Instead of down-to-earth Hannah, here was this black-haired gypsy, with eyes as big as cartwheels. How would they deal with her?

"I'll take you up and show you your room, Rebecca," Miss Miranda said. "Shut the door tight behind you. We don't want flies. Wipe your feet. Hang your hat and cape in the entry there as you go past. Lay your parasol in the entry closet."

"Do you mind if I keep them in my room, please? It always seems safer."

"There ain't any thieves around. Come along. Remember to always go up the back way. We don't use the front stairs on account of the carpet. Now look to your right and go in. When you've washed your face and hands and brushed your hair, you can come down. By and by we'll unpack your trunk and get you settled before supper."

Miranda stood studying the child. "Ain't you got your dress on backwards?" she said.

Rebecca looked at the row of buttons running down her chest. "Backwards? Oh, I see! No, that's all right. We're always buttoned up the front at our house. With seven children, Mother can't button and unbutton us all, you know, so this way we can do the buttons ourselves!"

Miranda frowned and said nothing as she closed the door.

Rebecca stood perfectly still in the center of the room and looked about her. There was a square of oilcloth in front of each piece of furniture. A rag rug lay beside the single bed, which was covered with a fringed white spread. Everything was as neat as wax. Far nicer than her room at the farm! It was a north-facing room. The long, narrow window looked out on the back buildings and the barn.

Rebecca didn't feel at all tired. But she did have a feeling she couldn't quite understand— part fear, part excitement. She stood her parasol in the corner. Then, in a rush of emotion, she tore off her hat, flung herself into the middle of the bed, and pulled the cover over her head.

In a moment the door opened and Miss Miranda entered without knocking.

"*Rebecca!*" she cried sternly.

A dark ruffled head and two frightened eyes appeared above the cover.

"What are you layin' on your good bed in the daytime for? You're messin' up the feathers, and dirtyin' the pillows with your dusty boots!"

Rebecca rose guiltily, knowing that she could not explain.

"I'm sorry, Aunt Miranda. Something came over me. I don't know what."

"Well, if it comes over you again very soon we'll have to find out what it is. Spread your bed up smooth this minute."

CHAPTER THREE

Sunday Letters

Dear Mother,
I am safely here. My dress didn't get too rumpled. I like Mr. Cobb very much. He throws newspapers strate to the doors. The brick house looks just the same as you have told us. The parler is splendid and gives you creeps and chills when you look in the door. The furnature is ellergant too, and all the rooms, but there are no good sitting-down places exsept in the kitchen. Aunt M. is not happy with me at all, but Aunt J. is kinder to me. She does not hate me as bad as Aunt M. does. Aunt J. gave me a dictionary to look up hard words in. That takes a good deal of time.

I am glad people can talk without stopping to spell. It is much eesier to talk than write and much more fun. Tell Mark he can have my paint box. I hope Hannah and John do not get tired doing my chores.

Your afectionate friend
Rebecca

p.s. Please give this poetry I wrote to John because he likes poetry even when it is not very good.

SUNDAY THOUGHTS
by Rebecca Rowena Randall

This house is dark and dull and drear
No light doth shine from far or near
    'Tis like a tomb.

My guardian angel is asleep
At least he doth no vigil keep
    But far doth roam.

Then give me back my lonely farm
Where none alive did wish me harm,
    Dear childhood home!

Dear Mother,

I am not happy this morning. Aunt M. was very cross and unfealing to me. Have I only been here a week? I wish Hannah had come instead of me for it was Hannah that they wanted and she is better than I am.

School is pretty good. I am smarter than Emma Jane Perkins and the other girls but not so smart as two boys. I am in the Sixth Reader. But just because I cannot say the Multiplication Table, Miss Dearborn threttens to put me in the baby class with the Simpson twins. I read with Dick Carter and Living Perkins, who are studying for the academy. Miss Dearborn teaches me grammer after the others have gone home.

I sew on brown gingham dresses every afternoon while Emma Jane and the Simpsons are playing. I can play from half past four to supper and after supper a little bit and Saturday afternoons. It is going to be a good year for apples and hay so you and John will be glad we can pay a little more of the morgage on the farm. Miss Dearborn asked us what is the object of edducation and I said the object of mine was to help pay off the morgage. She told Aunt M. and

I had to sew extra for punishment because she says a morgage is a disgrace like stealing or smallpox and it will be all over town that we owe money on our farm.

Sometimes I feer I cannot bare this life.
Your afectionate friend
Rebecca.

Dear John,
You remember when we tide the new dog in the barn how he bit the rope and howled? I am just like him only the brick house is the barn and I can not bite Aunt M. because I must be grateful and edducation is going to be the making of me and help you pay off the morgage when we grow up.
Your loving
Becky

CHAPTER FOUR

Sunshine in a Shady Place

Rebecca had started school right away in Riverboro, with only one month left in the school year. The little schoolhouse had a flagpole on top and stood on the crest of a hill. There were rolling fields and pine woods around it, and the river sparkled in the distance. But it was bare and ugly inside. There was an old black stove, a map of the United States, and two blackboards. On a corner shelf was a tin pail of drinking water with a long-handled dipper.

Miss Dearborn, the teacher, had a desk and chair on a platform. The twenty students sat on hard benches behind wooden desks.

Rebecca walked to school every morning. She loved this part of the day. She clasped her books in one hand, and her lunch pail swung from the other. She had blissful thoughts of the two soda biscuits spread with butter and syrup, the baked cup-custard, the doughnut, and the square of hard gingerbread in her lunch.

When the weather was fair, Rebecca and her new best friend, Emma Jane Perkins, took a short cut through the woods. They turned off the main road, crept through Uncle Josh Woodman's gate, and waved away Mrs. Carter's cows. They went down a well-worn path running through buttercups and sweet fern. They jumped from stone to stone across a brook. They went through a wood, climbed the steps of a wooden stile to get over another fence, went through a grassy meadow, slid under another gate, and came out into the road again.

At the last gate the two girls were met by some of the Simpson children. The Simpsons were poor and lived in a bleak house. Rebecca sympathized with the Simpsons. There were so many of them. They were covered in patches, just like her own family at Sunnybrook Farm.

It was fortunate that Rebecca had her books and her new friends, or she would have been unhappy that first summer after school ended. She made a great effort to please her grim and difficult Aunt Miranda. But her aunt's searching eyes, sharp voice, hard knotty fingers, thin straight lips, and long silences made it hard.

Rebecca irritated her aunt with every breath she drew. She forgot and used the front stairs because it was the shortest way to her bedroom. She left the dipper on the kitchen shelf instead of hanging it up over the pail. She sat in the chair the cat liked best. She was willing to go on errands, but often forgot what she was sent for. She left the screen doors open, and flies came in.

Aunt Jane was sunshine in a shady place to Rebecca. With her quiet voice and her kind eyes, she made Rebecca's life easier those first difficult weeks. Oh, those "brick house ways" were so hard to learn for this spirited little stranger!

Rebecca needed Aunt Jane's understanding as she struggled to sew dresses from endless yards of brown gingham. She broke the thread, pricked her finger, could not match the checks, and puckered the seams.

After Rebecca had been in Riverboro for several months—and after she had made several brown gingham dresses—she asked her Aunt Miranda if she might have another color for the next dress.

"I don't approve of children being rigged out in fancy colors, but I'll see what your Aunt Jane thinks," was the sharp reply.

"I think it would be all right to let Rebecca have one pink and one blue gingham," said Jane. "A child gets tired of sewing on one color. It's only natural she should long for a change. Besides, she'd look like a charity child always wearing the same brown. And brown looks dreadful on her!"

And so pink and blue gingham were ordered.

Rebecca worked her hardest on the pink dress. One afternoon, when she had nearly finished, Aunt Jane promised to make a pretty white trim for it. And she gave Rebecca permission to go and play with Emma Jane and Alice Robinson.

Rebecca leaped off the porch. She and her friends had several favorite places to play. The Simpsons had the most fascinating front yard in the village. It was filled with junk like old sleighs, broken couches, beds without headboards—

and never the same stuff on any two days. Mr. Abner Simpson spent little time with his family. He had a bad habit of trading off things belonging to his neighbors. So after every trade he generally spent some time in jail. Mrs. Simpson took in washing and the town helped in the feeding and clothing of the children.

Next to the Simpson yard there was a velvety stretch of ground beside a group of trees in the Sawyer pasture. The children brought pieces of wood from the sawmill to build houses there. They stored all their treasures in soapboxes: wee baskets and plates and cups, bits of broken china for parties, and dolls. They played out stories with their dolls in the playhouses—school, weddings, funerals, and tales from their books.

This afternoon they built a tall, square house around Rebecca. She was a romantic royal prisoner leaning against the bars of her prison. It was a wonderful experience standing inside the building with Emma Jane's apron wound about her hair, pretending to be a sad princess.

"I hate to have to take it down," said Alice, when it was time to go home. "It's been such a sight of work."

"If you just take off the top rows, I could step out," suggested the prisoner. "Then leave the stones, and you two can step down into the prison tomorrow."

"Maybe we could let the Simpson twins be the prisoners. We could pretend they steal things like their father does."

"They needn't steal just because their father does," argued Rebecca. "Don't you ever talk about it in front of them if you want to be my friends. My mother tells me never to say hard things about people's own folks to their face. She says nobody can bear it, and it's wicked to shame them for what isn't their fault."

CHAPTER FIVE

A Pink Dress and a Dark Storm

Fall came, and Rebecca settled back into school. Friday afternoons were her favorite. This was the time for plays, songs, and reciting poetry. Most of the students disliked all this. But Rebecca brought a new spirit into these afternoons. She taught Elijah and Elisha Simpson to recite funny poems, which delighted everyone. She found a poem with very few "S's" for Susan, who talked with a lisp.

Rebecca and Emma Jane had a short play ready for a certain Friday afternoon. Miss Dearborn said it was *so* good she had invited the doctor's wife, the minister's wife, two members of the school committee, and a few mothers to the program.

The teacher asked Living Perkins and Rebecca to decorate the blackboards. Living drew the map of North America. Rebecca chose to do an American flag in red, white, and blue chalk.

The students gave a round of cheers for the blackboards. At this, Rebecca's heart leaped for joy. She felt tears rising in her eyes, and could hardly see the way back to her seat. In her lonely little life she had never received applause. This was a wonderful, dazzling moment.

The students became wildly excited about the program and began fixing up the room. Huldah Meserve covered the largest holes in the plastered walls with pretty branches. The water pail was filled with wild flowers. Minnie Smallie covered the ugly stove with wild ferns.

Miss Dearborn let the children go to lunch early. Those who lived near enough could go home to change clothes. Emma Jane and Rebecca excitedly ran nearly every step of the way.

"Will your Aunt Miranda let you wear your best, or only your brown dress?" asked Emma Jane.

"I think I'll ask Aunt Jane," Rebecca replied. "Oh! If my pink was only finished! Aunt Jane was to make the trim and finish the buttonholes!"

Rebecca found the side door locked, but she knew the key was under the step. (So did everyone else in Riverboro.) She unlocked the door and went in to find her lunch on the table. A note from Aunt Jane said they had gone to the next town to shop. Rebecca swallowed a piece of bread and butter, and flew up the front stairs to her room. On the bed lay the pink gingham dress, finished by Aunt Jane's kind hands. Could she—dare she—wear it without asking? Wouldn't they want her to look her best for the important visitors?

"I'll wear it," she decided. "It's only gingham after all. It's *only* grand because it's new. Well... and it does have trimming on it. And it *is* pink."

She unbraided her pigtails and tied her hair back with a ribbon. She changed her shoes, then slipped on the pretty frock. Downstairs, she glanced in the parlor mirror and was delighted. She danced out the side door, and covered the mile between the brick house and school in an *incredibly* short time.

"Rebecca Randall!" exclaimed Emma Jane at the school door. "You're pretty as a picture!'

"I?" laughed Rebecca. "Nonsense! It's only the pink gingham."

"How on earth did you get your Aunt Miranda to let you put on your brand new dress?"

"They were both away," Rebecca responded. "I thought she might have said yes."

The afternoon was perfect. All the students did well. There were no failures, no tears, and every parent was proud. Not one child forgot a word of the verses.

Rebecca was ready and willing and never shy. Wherever she stood was the center of the stage. Her clear high voice soared above all the rest in the choruses. Everybody watched her and began to feel some of her eagerness. She didn't try to take all the glory for herself, but brought the other children into the fun.

As she walked home after school, it seemed to Rebecca that she could never be cool and calm again. There were thick clouds gathering in the sky, but she took no notice of them. Fears could not live in the joy that flooded her soul. She was walking on air—until she entered the side yard of the brick house. There was Aunt Miranda standing in the open doorway. With a rush, Rebecca came back to earth.

"Rebecca, I want to talk to you. What did you put on that good new dress for, on a school day, without permission?"

"I would have asked if you were at home," began Rebecca.

"You knew that I wouldn't have let you."

"If I'd been *certain* you wouldn't have let me I'd never have done it," said Rebecca. "But I wasn't *certain*. I thought perhaps you might, if you knew that the minister's wife and the doctor's wife and the school committee would all be at school. I haven't hurt my dress a mite, Aunt Miranda."

"It's the sneakiness of your actions that's the worst," said Miranda coldly. "And look at the other things you've done! You went up the front stairs! You didn't even hide your tracks, for you dropped your hankie on the way up. You left the screen out of your bedroom window for the flies to come in. You never cleared away your lunch and you left the side door unlocked. Why, *anyone* coulda come in and stolen what they liked!"

Rebecca sat down heavily in her chair as she heard the list of her crimes. How could she have been so careless? The tears began to flow now as she tried to explain.

"Oh, I'm so sorry!" she faltered. "I was decorating the schoolroom, and got late, and ran all the way home. It was hard getting into my dress alone, and I hadn't time to eat but a mouthful. And just at the last minute, when I honestly—*honestly*—would have thought about clearing away and locking up, I looked at the clock and knew I could hardly get back to school on time."

"Don't wail and carry on now. It's no good cryin' over spilt milk," answered Miranda. "An ounce of good behavior is worth a pound of regret. Instead of tryin' to see how little trouble you can make in a house that ain't your own home, it seems as if you tried to see how much you could put us out. Now you step upstairs, put on your nightgown, go to bed, and stay there till tomorrow mornin'. You'll find a bowl of crackers and milk on your bureau, and I don't want to hear a sound from you till breakfast time. Jane, run and take the dishtowels off the line and shut the shed doors. We're goin' to have a turrible storm."

"I think we've already *had* the storm," said Jane quietly.

Rebecca closed the door of her bedroom. With trembling fingers, she took off the beloved pink gingham. She dabbed her wet eyes to keep the tears off the lovely dress that she had worn at such a price. She smoothed it out carefully, pinched up the white ruffle at the neck, and laid it away with an extra little sob.

All the while a resolve was growing in her mind to leave the brick house and let Hannah come to Riverboro in her place.

She had thought Aunt Miranda might be pleased that she had done so well at school. But there was no hope of pleasing her in any way.

Rebecca decided she would go to Cousin Ann's in Maplewood on the stagecoach the next day with Mr. Cobb. She would slip away now and see if she could stay all night with the Cobbs and be off next morning before breakfast.

With Rebecca, to think was to act. She put on her oldest dress and hat and jacket. Then she wrapped her nightdress, comb, and toothbrush in a bundle and dropped it softly out of the window. She scrambled out of the window, caught hold of the lightning rod, jumped to the porch, used the ivy trellis for a ladder, and was soon flying up the road in the storm.

CHAPTER SIX

A Rainbow Bridge

Jeremiah Cobb sat at his lonely supper at the table by the kitchen window. "Mother" (as he called his wife) was nursing a sick neighbor. Mrs. Cobb was mother only to a little headstone in the churchyard, where their little Sarah Ann was buried. The loss of their only child gave them a special love for all children.

The rain still fell, and the heavens were dark. Looking up from his tea, the old man saw at the open door the very picture of misery. It was Rebecca, but he hardly recognized her. Her face was swollen with tears.

"Please, may I come in, Mr. Cobb?" she said.

His big heart went out to her. "Why, you're soakin' wet. I made a fire, hot as it was, thinkin' I wanted somethin' warm for my supper. There, we'll hang your soppy hat on the nail, an' put your jacket over the chair. An' then you turn your back to the stove an' dry yourself good."

"Oh, Mr. Cobb," Rebecca cried, "I've run away from the brick house. I want to go back to the farm. Will you keep me tonight and take me up to Maplewood in the stage? I haven't got any money for my fare, but I'll earn it somehow afterwards."

"Well, I guess we won't quarrel 'bout money, you and me," said the old man. "Come over here aside of me an' tell me all about it. Jest set down on that there wooden stool an' out with the whole story to Uncle Jerry."

Rebecca leaned her aching head against the patched, comforting knee and told her story. It was a tragic story for this young girl, but she told it truthfully.

Uncle Jerry stirred in his chair a good deal, muttering, "Poor little soul!"

"You will take me to Maplewood, won't you, Mr. Cobb?" begged Rebecca.

"Don't you fret a mite," he answered slowly. "Now draw up to the table and take a bite o' somethin' to eat, child. How'd you like to set in Mother's place an' pour me out another cup o' hot tea?"

Rebecca smiled faintly, and dried her eyes.

Mr. Cobb went on. "I suppose your mother will be turrible glad to see you back again?"

A tiny fear in the bottom of Rebecca's heart stirred and grew larger.

"She won't like it that I ran away, I s'pose. And she'll be right sorry that I couldn't please Aunt Miranda."

"I s'pose she was thinkin' o' your schoolin', lettin' you come down here. But land! You can go to school in Temperance, I s'pose?"

"Temperance only has two months of school."

"Oh, well! There's other things in the world beside edjercation," responded Uncle Jerry.

"Ye-es, though Mother thought that was going to be the making of me," returned Rebecca sadly.

"How is this school down here in Riverboro— pretty good?" inquired Uncle Jerry.

"Oh, it's a splendid school! And Miss Dearborn is a splendid teacher!"

"You like her, do you? Well, Mother was talkin' to her this afternoon. 'How does the girl from Temperance git along?' asks Mother. 'Oh, she's the best scholar I have!' says Miss Dearborn."

"Oh, Mr. Cobb, *did* she say that?" whispered Rebecca. "I've tried hard all the time, but I'll study the covers right off of the books now."

"You mean you would if you were to stay here," said Uncle Jerry. "Now ain't it too bad you've got to give it all up on account o' your Aunt Mirandy? Well, I can't hardly blame ya. She's cranky an' she's sour. An' I guess you ain't much on patience, are ya?"

"Not very much," replied Rebecca.

"I'm not sayin' you were in the wrong. But if you were to do over again... I'd say... Well, your Aunt Mirandy gives you clothes and food and schoolin'. And she *is* goin' to send you to the Academy in Wareham at a big expense. She's turrible hard to get along with... And she does kinda throw reminders at ya 'bout how she's helpin' ya. Throws 'em like bricks, I'd say. But she is helpin' ya just the same. Maybe it's *your* job to kinda pay for 'em in good behavior. Jane's a leetle bit more easy goin' than Mirandy, ain't she?"

"Oh, Aunt Jane and I get along splendidly," exclaimed Rebecca. "I like her better all the time. She likes me, too. And she understands."

"Jane will be real sorry to find you've gone away, I guess. But never mind. It can't be helped. She'll have a dull time with Mirandy—without your company. Mother declares she's never seen Jane look so young 'n' happy."

There was a silence in the little kitchen, except for the ticking of the tall clock and the beating of Rebecca's heart. The rain stopped, and a sudden rosy light filled the room. Outside the window, a rainbow arch spanned the heavens like a bridge.

"The shower's over," said the old man. "It's cleared the air. It's washed the face o' the earth nice an' clean. Everything tomorrow will shine like a new pin—when you an' I are drivin' upriver."

Rebecca rose from the table, and put on her hat and jacket. "I'm not going to drive upriver, Mr. Cobb," she said. "I'm going to stay here and—catch bricks. I don't know if Aunt Mirandy will take me in after I've run away, but I'm going back now while I have the courage. Would you be so good as to go with me, Mr. Cobb?"

"You'd better b'lieve your Uncle Jerry will," said the old man delightedly. "Now you've had all you can stand tonight, poor little soul. Mirandy will be sore an' cross, so I've got a plan. I'll drive you over to the brick house in my buggy. I'll git out an' git your Aunt Mirandy 'n' Aunt Jane out into the shed to plan for a load o' wood I'm sendin' them. You'll slip out and go upstairs to bed. You see, you ain't run away yet. You've only come over here to *talk* to me 'bout runnin' away. An' we've decided it ain't worth the trouble, right? Not much wrong in all that, is there, now?"

And so, they carried out Uncle Jerry's plan, and Rebecca sneaked in and went upstairs.

As she slipped into bed, she was aching and throbbing in every nerve. Even so, she felt a kind of peace stealing over her and she went to sleep.

"I've never seen a child improve in her work as Rebecca has today," remarked Miranda Sawyer to Jane on Saturday evening. "She *is* the beatin'est child! That settin' down I gave her was probably just what she needed. And I daresay it'll last for a month."

"I'm glad you're pleased," returned Jane. "But I think you want a cringing worm, not a bright, smiling child. When Rebecca came downstairs this morning it seemed to me she'd grown old in the night. If you'll let her go to the County Fair in Milltown with the Cobbs on Wednesday, that'll hearten her up a little."

Rebecca and Emma Jane *did* go to the Fair. And it was impossible for two children to see more, do more, and talk more than those two happy girls.

CHAPTER SEVEN

Rebecca's Punishment

Rebecca got on in the brick house as best she could that autumn. She stayed out of trouble, and therefore suffered no punishments. However, one event—one sad accident—actually made her decide she ought to punish herself.

Wearing her best dress, Rebecca had gone to take tea with the Cobbs. While crossing the bridge, she was taken by the beauty of the river. She leaned over the rail to enjoy the dashing waterfall beneath. Resting her elbows on the topmost board, she stood there dreaming.

What she did not know was that the bridge had just been painted.

The waterfall was a swirling wonder of water at any time of the year. It sparkled in summer sunshine. It shone cold and gray in November. It swelled and roared in April. Rebecca never went across the bridge without stopping to take in the beauty. And at this moment she was trying to write a poem—when she suddenly became aware of the wet paint.

"Oh! It's all over my best dress! Oh, what *will* Aunt Miranda say! Surely Mrs. Cobb can help me!" And she flew up the hill crying.

Mrs. Cobb calmly said she was able to remove almost any stain from almost any fabric. She dressed Rebecca in one of her blue robes. While they ate the evening meal, she dipped the dress in paint thinner.

When supper was cleared away, Rebecca washed the dishes. Mrs. Cobb worked on the dress, and Uncle Jerry offered advice from time to time. At length they left the dress to dry, and went into the sitting room.

Mrs. Cobb sat by her mending basket, and Uncle Jerry took down a gingham bag of snarled strings to unravel. Rebecca busied herself writing out the poem she had been working on.

When she had finished, Rebecca read her poem aloud. Oh, the praises! The Cobbs thought it was beautiful. Maybe even better than Mr. Longfellow's famous poems!

After a while they went into the kitchen to check on the dress. It was quite dry, and looked a little better—but the colors had run into streaks! Mrs. Cobb smoothed it with a warm iron. Rebecca put it on to see if the smudges showed.

They did.

Rebecca gave one look and sighed a deep sigh. "Well, goodnight. If I've got to have a scolding, I want it quick, and get it over," she said bravely. Then she left to go face Aunt Miranda.

"Poor little unlucky thing!" said Uncle Jerry. "I know she gets dreamy and all… but I vow, if she was ours, I'd let her slop paint all over the house before I could scold her."

Rebecca took her scolding like a soldier—and there *was* a lot of it. Aunt Miranda told her she would have to wear her dress, stained as it was, until it was worn out. Aunt Jane, who felt sorry for the child, promised to make her an apron to hide the streaks.

After Rebecca went to her room, she began to think of a way to punish herself. She must give up something, she decided. But, truth be told, she had very little to give. As she sat by the window, she looked about the room. There was hardly anything but the beloved pink parasol. Her eyes moved from the parasol... to outside the window... and down to the water well. That would do. She would fling her "dearest thing in life" into the depths of the water!

As usual, she took action right away. She stole out the front door, lifted the cover of the well, gave one sad shudder, and flung the little pink treasure down.

Rebecca felt refreshed the next morning. She had punished herself, and her little soul was uplifted. With a happy heart, she went to school.

Meanwhile, Miss Miranda tried to pump water from the well after breakfast—with no luck. She called in Mr. Flagg for help. He lifted the cover, explored a bit, and found the problem. An ivory "hook" had caught in the chain gear—a little parasol handle... Not only that, he had to clear out a bent and twisted pink parasol that had *somehow* opened and jammed in the well.

When Rebecca tried to explain why she had thrown her beloved pink parasol into Miranda Sawyer's well, she indeed sounded ridiculous— even to her own ears. How *could* she explain to a person who closed her lips into a thin line and looked at her out of blank eyes?

"Now see here, Rebecca," said Aunt Miranda. "When you think you ain't punished enough, just tell me. I'll come up with something more. Whatever it is, it'll be something that won't punish the whole family, and make 'em drink ivory dust, wood chips, and pink silk rags with their water."

CHAPTER EIGHT

Mr. Aladdin

Just before Thanksgiving, the poor Simpson home was in despair. There was little to eat, and less to wear. Many kind-hearted villagers brought food and clothes. But life was rather dull and dreary in the chill and gloom of November. The Simpson children knew that other people would soon have feasts of turkey, and golden pumpkin pies, and delicious stuffing.

They needed something to take their minds off all this. A pamphlet from the Excelsior Soap Company caught their attention. If they sold bars of soap, door to door, they could earn prizes! And so this is what they set upon doing.

They sold enough soap bars to earn a child's handcart. And the pamphlet had pictures of bigger and better prizes! Oh, how they wanted the beautiful brass banquet lamp with a lovely paper shade! But to earn such a lamp, they would have to sell soap to every village around! The problem was that only the oldest, Clara Belle, was any sort of a saleslady. So they talked to Rebecca and Emma Jane, and the girls promised to help.

On a Saturday, the girls drove the Perkins' old white horse to North Riverboro, three miles away. They put several boxes of soap into the back of the wagon to sell. It was a glorious Indian summer day, a rustly day, a scarlet and tan, yellow and bronze day. The air was like sparkling cider, and every field had its heaps of yellow and brown harvest, all ready for the barns or markets. The old horse sniffed the sweet bright air, and trotted like a colt.

At each house the girls took turns. One would hold the horse. The other took the soap samples to the housewife.

They had not sold much soap by the time they drew up to one gateway with a very large house set back off the road.

"It's your turn, Rebecca," said Emma Jane.

Rebecca walked toward the house with her head held high. On the porch she saw a good-looking young man sitting in a rocking chair. He had an air of the city about him. He had a well-shaven face, well-trimmed mustache, and well-fitting clothes. Rebecca felt shy, but she asked, "Is the lady of the house at home?"

"I am the lady of the house at present," said the stranger, with a smile. "What can I do for you?"

"Have you ever heard of the—I mean I would like to introduce to you a very remarkable soap. It is called Rose Red and Snow White. For bathing and washing clothes."

"Oh! I know that soap," said the gentleman. "Made out of pure vegetable fats, isn't it?"

"The very purest," agreed Rebecca.

"And yet a child could do the wash with it."

Rebecca felt lucky to find a customer who knew all good things about the soap already. She eagerly sat down on a stool at his side near the edge of the porch. Before long, she forgot all about Emma Jane! She was talking as if she had known the young man all her life.

"I'm just on a visit to my aunt," explained the delightful gentleman. "I used to stay here as a boy, and I love the spot."

"I don't think anything takes the place of one's childhood farm," said Rebecca quite seriously.

"So you think your childhood is a thing of the past, do you, young lady?"

"I can still remember it," answered Rebecca, "though it seems a long time ago."

"I can remember mine well enough, and an unpleasant one it was," said the stranger.

"So was mine," sighed Rebecca. "What was your worst trouble?"

"Too little food and clothes, mostly."

"Oh!" exclaimed Rebecca. "Mine was no shoes and too many babies and not enough books. But you're all right and happy now, aren't you?" She thought to herself that he *looked* handsome and successful. Yet she could see that his eyes were sad when he was not speaking.

"I'm doing pretty well, thank you. Now tell me, how much soap should I buy today?"

"How much would your aunt need?"

"Oh, I don't know. Soap keeps, doesn't it?"

"I'm not certain, but I think so."

"What are you going to do with the great profits you get from this business?" he asked.

Rebecca found herself describing the Simpson family, and their desperate need of a banquet lamp to brighten their lives.

"How many more do they need to sell?"

"If they sell two hundred more cakes this month and next, they can have the lamp by Christmas," Rebecca answered. "And a hundred more to get the lampshade by summer time."

"I see. Well, that's all right. I'll take three hundred cakes. That will give them shade and all."

At this remark, Rebecca tipped over and tumbled into a clump of lilac bushes!

The amused young man picked her up, set her on her feet, and brushed her off.

"You should never seem surprised when you have taken a large order," he said. "You ought to have replied 'Can't you make it three hundred and fifty?' instead of tipping over in that unbusinesslike way."

"But it doesn't seem right for you to buy so much. Are you sure you can afford it?"

"If I can't, I'll save on something else." He smiled. "What is your name, young lady?"

"Rebecca Rowena Randall, sir."

"Do you want to hear my name?"

"I think I know already," answered Rebecca, with a bright glance. "I'm sure you must be Mr. Aladdin in *The Arabian Nights*—with the magic lamp that grants wishes! Oh, I must run down and tell Emma Jane."

Mr. Aladdin followed Rebecca to the wagon and took the soap.

"If you could keep a secret, it would be a nice surprise to have the lamp arrive at the Simpsons' on Thanksgiving Day, wouldn't it?" he asked.

They gladly agreed, and thanked him over and over. Tears of joy stood in Rebecca's eyes.

"Oh, don't mention it!" laughed Mr. Aladdin. "I like to see a thing well done. Good-bye, Miss Rebecca Rowena! Just let me know whenever you have anything to sell. I'm certain I shall want to buy it."

CHAPTER NINE

The Banquet Lamp

There was company at the brick house for Thanksgiving dinner. The Burnham sisters, from North Riverboro, had spent the holiday with the Sawyer sisters for the past twenty-five years.

Rebecca sat silent with a book after the dishes were washed. When it was nearly five she asked if she could go to the Simpsons'.

"The Simpsons have a new lamp!" said Rebecca. "The children got it as a prize for selling soap. And Emma Jane and I promised to go see it lighted and make it a kind of party."

"Well, you can go for a while, I s'pose," sniffed Aunt Miranda. "Seein' as it's Thanksgiving."

After she left, the Burnham sisters said that Rebecca had improved greatly since coming to the brick house.

"There's plenty of room left for improvement," answered Miranda. "Land, she's into everything! Gone to see a lamp! I didn't think those *Simpson* children had brains enough to sell anything."

"One of them must have," said Ellen Burnham. "The girl that was selling soap at the Ladds' home in North Riverboro—well now, Adam Ladd said she was the most remarkable child he ever saw."

"It must have been Clara Belle. And I would never call her remarkable," answered Miss Miranda. "Has Adam been home again?"

"Yes, he's been staying a few days with his aunt. There's no limit to the money he's making, they say. And to think we can remember the time he was a barefoot boy without two shirts to his name! It is strange he hasn't married, with all his money. And him so fond of children! He always has a pack of them at his heels."

"There's hope for him still, though," said Miss Jane. "He's just a young man."

"He could get a wife in Riverboro if he was a hundred and thirty," remarked Miss Miranda.

"Adam's aunt says he was so taken with the girl that sold the soap that he declared he was going to bring her a Christmas present," Miss Ellen went on. "He remarked about this child's handsome eyes. He said it was her eyes that made him buy the three hundred cakes."

The conversation made Jane nervous. What child in Riverboro could be described as remarkable and winning, *except Rebecca*? What child had wonderful eyes, *except Rebecca*? And finally, was there ever a child in the world who could make a man buy soap by the hundred cakes, *except Rebecca*?

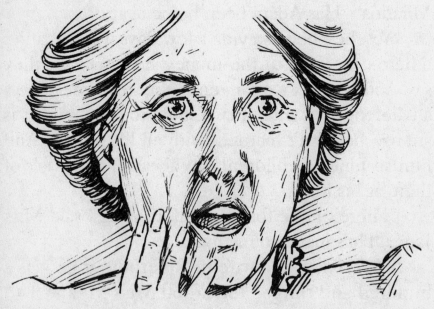

Meantime, the "remarkable" child had flown up the road in the deepening dusk. In a moment she was met by Emma Jane.

"I have a handful of nuts and raisins and some apples," said Rebecca.

"I have peppermints and maple sugar," said Emma Jane. "And the doctor gave them sweet potatoes and cranberries and turnips! Father sent a roast. And Mrs. Cobb gave them a chicken and a jar of mincemeat!"

At five-thirty, the Simpson house was a festive scene! The lamp itself seemed to be having the party and receiving the guests. The children had taken the one small table in the house and placed it in the far corner of the room. And on it stood the magical lamp!

Mrs. Simpson put the fire out. The lamp was lit. The brass glistened like gold. The red paper shade glowed like a giant ruby. The lamp flung a wide splash of light upon the floor. And in that soft light sat all the Simpson children in awe and solemn silence. Emma Jane and Rebecca stood behind them, hand in hand. No one spoke. The scene was too thrilling and serious for that.

When it was time for Rebecca and Emma Jane to go, Clara Belle said, "I'm so glad you both live where you can see it shine from our windows. I wonder how long it will burn without bein' filled? We don't have much kerosene."

"Oh, yes, we do!" cried Seesaw Simpson. "There's a great barrel of it settin' out in the shed! Mr. Tubbs brought it and said somebody sent an order by mail for it."

Rebecca squeezed Emma Jane's arm. "It must have been Mr. Aladdin," she whispered.

Rebecca entered the brick house dining room joyously. The Burnham sisters had gone and the two aunts were knitting.

"It was a heavenly party," she cried, taking off her hat and cape.

"Go back and see if you have shut the door tight, and then lock it," said Miss Miranda.

"And the lamp is lovely," said Rebecca, coming in again. "Aunt Jane, Aunt Miranda! Come into the kitchen and look out of the sink window. You can see it shining all red!"

Aunt Jane followed Rebecca into the kitchen.

"Rebecca, who was it that sold the three hundred cakes of soap to Mr. Ladd?"

"Mr. *Who?*" exclaimed Rebecca.

"Adam Ladd."

"Is *that* his real name? I didn't make a bad guess. Aladdin sounds like Adam Ladd, doesn't it!" Rebecca laughed softly to herself.

"Answer me, Rebecca."

"Oh! Emma Jane and I sold it. He needed the soap as a present for his aunt."

"I really wish you wouldn't do anything out of the ordinary without asking Mirandy first. You do such very odd things."

"There can't be anything wrong this time," Rebecca answered confidently. "Ever since we sold the soap, I have felt as if the banquet lamp was inside of me, all lighted up."

Rebecca's eyes were brilliant, and her cheeks were rosy. Her loose hair lightly tumbled in waves over her forehead.

"That's just the way you look, Rebecca—for all the world as if you *did* have a lamp burning inside of you," sighed Aunt Jane. "Rebecca! Rebecca! I wish you could take things easier, child. I am fearful for you sometimes."

On Christmas Day, Rebecca had exchanged gifts with her aunts when a knock came on the door. She was handed a package with her name on it. She took it like one in a dream and carried it into the dining room.

"It's a present. It must be," she said, looking at it in a dazed sort of way. "But I can't think who it could be from."

"A good way to find out would be to open it," remarked Miss Miranda.

Rebecca opened it with trembling fingers. Inside a pretty case was a long chain of pink coral beads with a cross made of coral rosebuds. A card with "Merry Christmas from Mr. Aladdin" lay under the cross. A silver chain with a blue locket was marked for Emma Jane. The card read:

Dear Miss Rebecca Rowena,
I hope I have chosen the right gifts for you and your friend. You must wear your chain this afternoon, please, for I am coming over in my new sleigh to take you both for a drive. My aunt is delighted with the soap.
Sincerely, your friend,
Adam Ladd

"Well, well!" cried Miss Jane. "Isn't that kind of him? Now eat your breakfast, Rebecca. After we've washed up the dishes you can run on over to Emma's and take her chain. What's the matter, child?"

Rebecca's joy was too deep for words. Tears filled her eyes and slowly fell down her cheeks.

Adam Ladd called as he promised, and met the two aunts. Rebecca wore her lovely pink coral necklace, and happiness and excitement filled her soul. The sleigh ride was the crowning moment of that glorious Christmas Day. Rebecca went to sleep many nights afterward with the precious coral chain under her pillow—with one hand on it to be certain that it was safe.

CHAPTER TEN

Seasons of Change

The next year or two brought growth and change for Rebecca. She did well in school and, for the most part, kept out of trouble. As Rebecca grew, her friends did also. Some left Riverboro. Dick Carter, Living Perkins, and Huldah Meserve enrolled in the Academy in Wareham. The Simpsons moved away. Rebecca and Emma Jane remained the best of friends. Yet, still, there was an emptiness inside her. She longed for a special friend who would understand what she felt in her heart. Emma Jane was dear, but she did not enjoy poetry and did not feel the rushes of joy that Rebecca could feel.

"Uncle Jerry" and "Aunt Sarah" Cobb were good friends. The sight of old Uncle Jerry always made Rebecca's heart warm. She often helped the old man dig potatoes or shell beans. And she sometimes stayed with him while he did his evening milking. He was the only person to whom she poured out her whole heart. He would listen to her hopes and dreams.

At the brick house, Rebecca practiced her scales and exercises on the old piano. But at the Cobbs' cabinet organ she sang like a bird. Here she was happy and loved. Still, she longed for somebody who not only loved but also understood her. Perhaps in the big world of Wareham there would be people who thought and dreamed and wondered as she did.

Rebecca shot up like a young tree. Aunt Jane could no longer let down her hems, and Aunt Miranda had to agree that new dresses were needed. Rebecca's old dresses were sent to Sunnybrook Farm to be made over for Jenny.

News came every month from Sunnybrook Farm. Rebecca's favorite brother, John, had his heart set on becoming a country doctor. Cousin Ann's husband had died, and John had gone to live with her. He was to have good schooling and the use of the old doctor's medical library. In return, he would care for the horse and cow and barn. There was a rumor that the new railroad might go near Sunnybrook Farm, and the land would rise in value. This was good news!

But there was sad news, too. Little Mira, the youngest child, had died. Rebecca went home for a sorrowful two-week visit. There she wept over a little grave under a willow tree at Sunnybrook Farm. Her mother was sad. The house was sad. All the years of penny-pinching and being poor seemed to add to the sadness. Especially for Rebecca, who was so sensitive to life and beauty.

Rebecca walked through all her familiar, secret places. There was the spot where the Indian pipes grew. The marshy ground where the flowers were largest and bluest. The maple tree where she found the oriole's nest. The hedge where the field mice lived. The moss-covered stump where the white toadstools sprang up as if by magic. And the hole at the root of the tall pine where an old toad made his home. These were the landmarks of her childhood, and she looked at them as across an endless distance.

Even the dear little brook was sad. In summer the merry stream had danced over white pebbles on its way to deep pools where it could be still and think. Now, like Mira, it was cold and quiet, wrapped in its shroud of snow. Rebecca knelt and put her ear to the glaze of ice. She imagined she could hear a faint, tinkling sound. It was all right! Sunnybrook would sing again in the spring. Perhaps Mira, too, would have her singing time somewhere.

CHAPTER ELEVEN

Rebecca Represents the Family

Rebecca was in her last year in the Riverboro school. She was thirteen and looking forward to going to the Academy in Wareham the next fall. She and Emma Jane, and other Riverboro schoolmates, would take the train to the bustling town—just like grown adults!

In March, Rebecca had a chance to show her aunts that the "wild little gypsy" was growing into a young lady. The church had a meeting for the visit of the Reverend Amos Burch and his family. They were missionaries returning from Syria. Both Miranda and Jane had taken bad colds, so Miranda sent Rebecca to represent the family.

At the church, Rebecca was asked to play the organ. Like a little adult, she agreed. Then Mr. Burch gave an inspiring talk on the work they were doing in Syria. It was so fascinating that many asked if he could talk more about how the people in Syria lived. Mr. Burch said he would the next evening—that is, if someone would let his family stay overnight.

There was a long, embarrassing silence.

Mrs. Robinson leaned over to Rebecca. "Your grandfather *always* entertained the missionaries when he was alive," she whispered.

She meant this for a stab at Miss Miranda, who did not like company. But Rebecca thought it was a suggestion. If it had been a former custom, perhaps her aunts would want her to do the right thing. And she *was* representing the family. Rebecca stood up straight and tall and invited the family to the brick house.

At home, Aunt Miranda was upset. "Explain, if you can, who gave you the right to invite strangers to stay here overnight? You know we ain't had any company for twenty years. And I don't intend to have any for another twenty—or at any rate while I'm the head of the house."

"Don't blame her, Miranda, till you've heard her story," said Jane.

Nervously, Rebecca explained. "Mrs. Robinson whispered to me that the missionaries *always* used to go to the brick house when grandfather was alive. So I thought I ought to invite them, since you weren't there to do it for yourself. Mr. Burch prayed for Grandfather, and called him a man of God, and thanked our Heavenly Father that his spirit was still alive in his daughters (that was you). And he was so glad that the good old brick house— where so many *other* preachers and missionaries had been helped—was still open for the stranger and traveler."

A gate in Miranda's heart swung open a little on its stiff and rusty hinges. Memories came to her of the old days and her beloved father.

"Well, I see you did the right thing, Rebecca," she said quietly.

"Now, since you're both sick, couldn't you trust me just once to get ready?" Rebecca asked.

"I believe I will," sighed Miranda. "I'll lay down and see if I can get strength to cook supper. It's half past three—don't you let me lay a minute past five, Rebecca."

Rebecca dashed upstairs like a whirlwind. The aunts could hear her scurrying to and fro, fluffing pillows and feather beds, flapping towels, and singing while she worked.

When she called her aunts at five o'clock, everything was ready. The missionary family arrived promptly, and Rebecca took over the care of their two little girls. There was a fine supper and a pleasant evening with members of the church who came in. The Burches told strange and beautiful stories about Syria. The two children sang, while Rebecca played the old piano for them.

At eight, Rebecca said, in her most grown-up voice, "Time for *little* missionaries to go upstairs!" The children said goodnight, and Rebecca took them up to bed.

Rebecca woke up before six the next morning, and quickly put on a robe and slippers. She stole quietly down the "forbidden" front stairs. Carefully, she closed the kitchen door behind her so that no noise would waken the rest of the household. She busied herself for a half-hour, getting breakfast ready. Then she went back to her room to dress before calling the children.

When Miranda and Jane opened the kitchen door, they stared in wonder. Had they strayed into the wrong house by mistake?

There was a roaring fire in the stove. The teakettle was singing and bubbling. A rich, welcoming scent came from the coffeepot. The potatoes and corned beef were on the wooden tray. The brown and white loaves were out. The toast rack was ready, the milk was skimmed, and the butter had been brought from the dairy.

Miranda and Jane exchanged glances.

"Ain't she the beatin'est child that ever was born into the world!" exclaimed Miranda. "But she can work when she's got a mind to! I declare she's all Sawyer!"

The day and the evening went by pleasantly. The Burches left with lively hearts and many thanks. Afterward, Miranda's feelings toward "the beatin'est child" were softer, though she didn't show them.

Later in life, Rebecca would look back on this visit with the Burches with pride. It was the first time she was asked to represent the family. She had done it well—and she had done it with love. It was a turning point in her life.

Have you ever noticed how gracious and mannerly you feel when you wear a beautiful new dress? Or how quiet and serious you feel when you close your eyes, clasp your hands, and bow your head? Or how good you feel when you listen politely to another person? Then you know how your actions—and how you stand and look— can change how you feel on the inside. And you know how Rebecca felt. She had *acted* grown up, so she *became* grown up.

CHAPTER TWELVE

School in Wareham

The day finally came! Rebecca and Emma Jane enrolled at Wareham Academy. They went on the train every day September to Christmas. Then they boarded in a rooming house in Wareham during the three coldest months. Aunt Miranda agreed to pay this expense.

Wareham was different from Riverboro—as different as Riverboro had been from Sunnybrook Farm. It was a pretty village with a broad main street shaded by great maples and elms. It had a drugstore, a blacksmith, a plumber, several shops and churches, and many boardinghouses. Life in the village centered on the Academy.

High school lasted four years, but Rebecca planned to finish in three years. She wanted to begin earning a living by the time she was seventeen. That way, she could help send her younger brothers and sisters to school. Emma Jane was not a good student, and could have stayed in Riverboro to finish. But she wanted to stay with Rebecca, so her parents agreed to let her go. Loyalty, after all, is as valuable in this world as brains and talent.

Rebecca studied English literature and writing with her favorite teacher, Miss Emily Maxwell. One day, Miss Maxwell asked each new student to bring her an essay written at their old school. Rebecca stayed after class and came shyly up to Miss Maxwell's desk.

"Miss Maxwell, I can bring you an old essay, but they were all bad. I never did like the topics we had to write about. I can't bear to show them. May I bring my poetry instead?"

Miss Maxwell agreed to look at the poetry. Rebecca left copies with her, and Miss Maxwell took them home to read, along with essays from the other students. A few days afterward she asked Rebecca to stay after class.

The room was quiet. Red leaves rustled in the breeze and flew in at the open window. Miss Maxwell sat by Rebecca's side on the bench.

"Did you think these were good?" she asked.

"Not so very," confessed Rebecca, "but it's hard to tell all by yourself."

Miss Maxwell decided that Rebecca would prefer the truth. "Well," she said smiling, "you were right. Your poetry needs some work."

"Then I must give up all hope of ever being a writer!" sighed Rebecca. "Must I never try any more poetry?"

"You have a natural sense of rhyme and meter, Rebecca. You should keep trying. When you are older, I think you may write very good verses. Poetry needs knowledge and vision, experience and imagination, Rebecca. You have a great deal of imagination and vision and the rest will come. You'll enjoy the first essay. I'm going to ask all the new students to write a letter to their family telling of their town and school life."

"Do I have to write it as *myself*?" asked Rebecca.

"What do you mean?"

"Well, you see, if I write a letter from Rebecca Randall to her sister Hannah at Sunnybrook Farm the letter would have to be rather dull. But now, if I could make believe I was a *different* girl, and could write to someone who could understand everything I said, I could make it nicer."

"I think that's a delightful plan," said Miss Maxwell. "And whom will you pretend to be?"

"A noble, rich girl with golden hair! She has come to live in Wareham where her father lived when he was a boy, long before he made his fortune. The father is dead now, and she has a guardian, the best and kindest man in the world. He is sometimes very quiet and serious, but sometimes happy and full of fun. I shall call her Evelyn! And her guardian's name shall be Mr. Adam Ladd."

"Do you *know* Mr. Ladd?" asked Miss Maxwell in surprise.

"Yes, he's my very best friend," cried Rebecca delightedly. "Do you know him, too?"

"Oh, yes. He is a trustee of this school, you know. He often comes here. I'm sure he will enjoy a letter from 'Evelyn' if I may show it to him."

Rebecca said yes.

Miss Maxwell soon reported to Adam Ladd that she had found a pearl in his young friend. Adam agreed heartily.

CHAPTER THIRTEEN

A Heart in Bloom

"How d'ye *do*, girls?" chirped Huldah Meserve. She peeped into Rebecca and Emma Jane's room one Friday. "Oh, *do* stop studying a minute and show me your room! It's simply too cute for words! I don't know what gives it that simply *gorgeous* look. Is it Rebecca's lamp? Or that elegant screen? You certainly do have it looking good."

"Isn't this your study hour?" Rebecca asked. She was a little upset at being bothered.

"Yes, but I *had* to go downtown for some gloves. And then I went to the principal's office to see if my Latin grammar book that I lost had been handed in. That's the reason I'm dressed *so* fine."

Huldah was stylish and she flirted with any boy who was near. Today she was wearing a sporty blue woolen dress with a gray jacket. Her gray felt hat had a white tissue veil with large black dots. It made her delicate skin look brilliant. Her open jacket showed several society pins to prove how popular she was.

"There was a perfectly elegant gentleman in the principal's office," Huldah went on, dancing into the room. "He was a stranger to me. He was handsome as a picture and had on a stylish suit of clothes. His only jewelry was a cameo scarf pin and a perfectly *gorgeous* ring—it wound round and round his finger. Oh dear, I must run! There's the class bell!"

A ring that wound round the finger? Rebecca knew that ring. Mr. Aladdin wore one like it. Her *own* Mr. Aladdin, who was so kind and generous to her. Every Christmas he gave her and Emma Jane a special gift. He had called several times at the brick house to say hello to her aunts. Sometimes he wrote from Boston and asked her the news of Riverboro. She would send him pages of gossip. If Huldah's "stranger" turned out to be Mr. Aladdin, would he come to see her?

On Fridays, Rebecca always spent a few hours at Miss Maxwell's home before she caught the train to Riverboro. And so today she ran down the path through the pine woods to the large white house on a quiet village street. The maid knew to take her to Miss Maxwell's library room. She could wait there for Miss Maxwell to come from class for a half-hour of talk.

She selected *David Copperfield* and sank into a seat by the window. When she had read for half an hour, she glanced out of the window. Whom should she see but Huldah coming from the path through the woods *with Mr. Aladdin!* Huldah was holding her skirts daintily. She was stepping lightly in her very grown-up high-heeled shoes. Her cheeks were glowing, and her eyes were sparkling under the black and white veil.

Rebecca slipped from her seat by the window to the rug before the bright fire. She leaned her head on the seat of the great easy chair. There was a strange storm in her heart, and it frightened her. She never minded that Emma Jane was part of her friendship with Mr. Aladdin. Yet she could not bear to give up any part of that friendship to *Huldah.*

Suddenly the door opened quietly. "Miss Maxwell told me I should find Miss Rebecca Randall here."

Rebecca was startled by the sound and sprang to her feet. "Mr. Aladdin!" she said joyfully. "Oh! I knew you were in Wareham, and I was afraid you wouldn't have time to see me."

"But I will always make time for you, Rebecca."

The light in the room grew softer, the fire crackled cheerily. They talked of many things, for they had not seen each other for months. Rebecca asked him how he came to be a trustee of the Wareham Academy.

"My mother used to be a trustee of the school. Several years after she died, I accepted the position in her memory. Her last happy years were spent here. She was married a month after she graduated, and she lived only until I was ten. Would you like to see my mother, Rebecca?"

He handed Rebecca a leather case. She took it gently and opened it. Inside was an innocent, pink-and-white daisy of a face that went straight to the heart.

"Oh, what a sweet, sweet, flowery face!" she whispered softly.

"The bitter weather of the world bent the flower and dragged it to the earth. She died for lack of love and care. I was only a child and could do nothing to protect her. All that I have gained in life seems, now and then, so useless—since I cannot share it with her!"

Rebecca was seeing a new Mr. Aladdin. Her heart gave a throb of understanding and sympathy. This explained the tired look in his eyes, under the laughter.

"I'm so glad I know," she said, "and so glad I could see her just as she was then. I wish she could have been kept happy, and had lived to see you grow up strong and good. She would have been so proud to know how you turned out. But... perhaps she *does* know."

"You are a comforting little person, Rebecca," said Adam, rising from his chair.

Rebecca rose, too. Small tears were trembling on her lashes. The young man looked at her suddenly as if with new eyes.

"Why, little Rose Red-Snow White is making way for a new girl!" he said. He took her slim brown hands in his. "I believe you are becoming a young lady!"

"Oh, Mr. Aladdin!" cried Rebecca "I am not fifteen yet. It will be three years before I'm a young lady of seventeen!"

"Rebecca," he said, after a moment's pause, "who is that young girl with a lot of pretty red hair and very fancy manners? She walked with me down the hill. Do you know whom I mean?"

"It is Huldah Meserve."

Adam put a finger under Rebecca's chin and looked into her clear eyes.

"Don't form yourself on her, Rebecca," he said seriously. "Clover blossoms that grow in the fields beside Sunnybrook must not be tied in the same bouquet with showy sunflowers. They are too sweet and fragrant and wholesome."

CHAPTER FOURTEEN

Aladdin Grants Some Wishes

Rebecca studied all during her summer vacation. On her return in the autumn, she passed special exams. This would allow her to finish in two more years. She wasn't a remarkable scholar, but her bright, imaginative answers delighted her teachers.

By the spring of the second year, she had become a leader at the school—just as she had been in Riverboro. She was elected assistant editor of the Wareham Academy newspaper. She was the first girl to have that position.

"She'll always get votes," said Huldah Meserve. "I only wish *I* was tall and dark-haired and had the gift of making people believe I could do great things, like Rebecca Randall. There's one thing though. The boys call her pretty, but you notice they don't really give her much attention."

Rebecca *was* pretty. The boys *did* notice her. But Rebecca just did not have much interest in boys—even for fifteen and a half!

Rebecca's studies kept her very busy. She still had to worry about the difficult problems of daily living. *And* she was very concerned about matters at the brick house and at the farm.

During the autumn and winter of that year, Rebecca felt as if Aunt Miranda was even more grumpy and picky. She seemed to find fault with Rebecca at every turn.

One Saturday, Rebecca had run upstairs to Aunt Jane and burst into a flood of tears. "Aunt Jane," she exclaimed, "sometimes I think I can't stand Aunt Miranda's constant scolding. Nothing I can do suits her."

Aunt Jane cried with Rebecca as she tried to soothe her. "You must be patient," she said. She wiped away Rebecca's tears, and then her own. "I haven't told you, for I didn't want to trouble you when you're studying so hard... but your Aunt Miranda isn't well. One Monday morning about a month ago, she had what the doctor thought was a little stroke. She's failing right along, and that's what makes her so fretful."

Rebecca stopped crying. "Oh, the poor dear thing! I won't mind a bit what she says now. Perhaps it won't be as bad as you think."

Things were not well at Sunnybrook Farm, either. The time for paying the interest on the mortgage had come and gone. For the first time in fourteen years, they did not have the forty-eight dollars to pay the bank.

The only happy news from Sunnybrook Farm was Hannah's engagement to marry Will Melville. He was a young farmer with land right next to Sunnybrook. Hannah was blissful and excited. However, she was *so* happy, she never gave a thought to her own mother's worries. And she gave no thought to earning any money to help pay on the mortgage.

One cold spring day, Adam Ladd was driving through the Boston streets. In a shop window he saw a rose-colored parasol. It reminded him of Rebecca. She had once told him about *another* little pink parasol that had met a tragic end. He bought the parasol and sent it to Wareham at once. Then, an hour later he realized he had not thought of Emma Jane! He returned quickly to buy a blue parasol.

He sometimes went to Temperance now on business. There was a new railroad being built, and he was on the planning board. Every land owner hoped the tracks would go through *their* land, for the railroad would pay quite a bit of money for the land. There was a chance that the tracks would go through Sunnybrook Farm. If they did, Mrs. Randall would be well paid.

Adam Ladd came to Wareham one day straight from Temperance. While he was there, he had a long walk and talk with Rebecca. He noticed that she was looking pale and thin.

She wore her long black braids wrapped about her head. Her front hair framed her face in loose waves. Adam looked at her in a way that made her put her hands over her face and laugh through them shyly.

"I know what you are thinking, Mr. Aladdin," she said. "That my dress is an inch longer than last year, and my hair different. But I'm not nearly a young lady yet. Sixteen is a month off still."

He only responded by saying that perhaps she was studying too hard. But after a little more talk, he realized why she looked so tired. She was worried about the overdue payment on the farm.

After their talk, Adam went to the principal's office. He told the principal that he wanted to sponsor an essay contest for the older students. He would give cash prizes. To himself he thought: *If Rebecca could win—and she is a fine writer—she could pay the debt on the farm.*

Then Adam visited Miss Maxwell.

"Miss Maxwell, doesn't it strike you that our friend Rebecca looks awfully tired?"

"She does indeed," agreed Miss Maxwell. "And I plan to take her with me to my favorite retreat, at spring vacation."

"What a wonderful idea. But, let me help with her traveling costs. I can only give her such help through you. I am greatly interested in Rebecca, and have been for some years."

"Oh, but don't pretend *you* discovered her," said Miss Maxwell warmly, "for I did that myself."

"She was a dear friend of mine long before she came to Wareham," laughed Adam. "Are you planning to take Emma Jane also?"

"No. I prefer to have Rebecca all to myself."

"I can understand that," he said, without thinking. "I mean, of course!" he added hastily. "One person is easier to travel with than two."

Here they saw Rebecca walking down the quiet street with a lad of sixteen. They were reading something aloud to each other. Their heads were bent close together over a sheet of paper. Rebecca kept glancing up at the boy, her eyes sparkling.

"I don't think that I believe boys and girls should be in the same school!" Adam said, looking unhappy.

Miss Maxwell smiled at his jealousy, and added quickly, "You are watching the senior and the junior editors of the school newspaper, *The Pilot*, walking together!"

CHAPTER FIFTEEN

The Gates of Childhood

The vacation with Miss Maxwell was more than Rebecca could imagine! She had her first glimpse of the ocean. The strange new scenes and the freedom thrilled her. She had always hungered for new things to see and learn. She loved life and thirsted for beauty. She had a great need for the music and the poetry of life! Now life had grown all at once rich and sweet, wide and full.

Miss Maxwell told her of the essay contest, and this stayed on her mind. Oh! She could never be happy unless she won it. How proud Mr. Aladdin would be! She came back from her vacation with many new ideas and thoughts for it.

The summer term ended and graduation was held for Huldah Meserve, Dick Carter, Living Perkins, and the other seniors. At graduation the essay winners were announced. Huldah received second prize. But the first prize went to Rebecca, who wasn't even a senior yet! She immediately took the money to her mother at Sunnybrook Farm to pay the mortgage interest.

Hannah had married Will already. So Rebecca stayed for a while to help her mother adjust to managing the farm without Hannah.

Back at school, her last year seemed to go by like a fast train, and graduation day soon dawned. Rebecca stole softly out of bed, crept to the window, threw open the blinds, and welcomed the rosy light. Somehow, even the sun looked different on this special day—larger, redder, more important than usual.

Parents and relatives of the seniors had been coming on the train and driving into town since breakfast time. Lines of buggies and wagons were drawn up along the sides of the shady roads. The streets were filled with people wearing their best clothes. The female seniors were seated in their bedrooms, while mothers hovered over them.

The mothers combed and fussed and fixed hair ribbons. Then the girls slipped on the prettiest dotted or white Swiss muslin dresses. Rebecca couldn't afford Swiss muslin. She and Emma Jane had dresses of plain white muslin trimmed with fine hand stitching.

The two girls waited in their room alone. Emma Jane was rather tearful, for this was the last day they would be together. Rebecca had been offered two positions, and surely she would choose one and move away. One position was as a piano teacher at a girl's boarding school in Augusta. The other was an assistant's place in the Edgewood High School. The pay was not much for either position. Rebecca liked the music teacher job, for she could practice her music while she taught.

Rebecca grew more excited as the day went on. When the first bell rang through the halls, she took in a breath. In five minutes the class would line up for graduation! She stood at the window, speechless, with her hand on her heart.

"It is coming, Emmie. We are closing the gates of childhood behind us. I can almost see them swing. I can almost hear them clang. And I can't tell whether I am glad or sorry."

"I don't care how they swing or clang," said Emma Jane, "as long as we're are on the same side of the gate. But we won't be. I know we won't!"

"Emmie, don't you dare cry! For I'm just on the brink myself! If only you were graduating with me. That's my only sorrow. Hug me once for luck, dear Emmie."

Ten minutes later, Adam Ladd came into the main street and stopped to watch the graduates stride down the road to the meeting house. He stood under the elms in the old village street where his mother had walked so many years before. He was just turning toward the church when he heard a little sob. Behind a hedge in the garden was a forlorn person in white.

He stepped inside the gate and said, "What's wrong, Miss Emma?"

"Oh, is it you, Mr. Ladd? Rebecca wouldn't let me cry, but I must. I'm not graduating with Rebecca! Not that I mind that. I just can't stand being separated from Becky!"

The two walked together along the street and into the church, while Adam tried to comfort the sad girl. Rebecca waved and smiled when she saw them sitting together.

Rebecca also saw Hannah and Will with John and Cousin Ann. She felt a pang that her mother could not leave the farm, even for this day. But she smiled again when she saw the Cobbs. No one could fail to see Uncle Jerry. He was so thrilled and didn't even try to hide his tears. He had told *every* neighbor about the marvelous graduate whom he had known ever since she was a child.

There were other Riverboro faces, but where was Aunt Jane? Rebecca knew that Aunt Miranda could not come, but where, on this day of days, was her beloved Aunt Jane? However, this thought came and went in a flash as the day's events began. She played the piano, she sang, she recited the prayer like one in a dream.

And then… it was over! The diplomas were presented with a wild round of applause for each graduate. After the crowd had thinned a little, Adam Ladd made his way to the platform.

Rebecca met him in the aisle. "Oh, Mr. Aladdin, I am so glad you could come! Tell me"— and she looked at him half shyly—"tell me, Mr. Aladdin—did I do all right?"

"More than all right!" he said warmly. "I'm glad I met the girl. I'm proud I know the young lady."

Adam left the church and came upon Miss Maxwell. They always *did* seem to end up talking about Rebecca, and this day was no different.

"I believe that happier days are dawning for her," said Adam. "You must keep this a secret, but Mrs. Randall's farm will be bought by the new railroad. She will receive six thousand dollars. That's not a fortune, but she'll make three to four hundred dollars a year, if she will let me invest it for her."

"Then Rebecca won't be burdened with debt on the farm," said Miss Maxwell softly. "That is as it should be. For she has talent. She has a future. And she must follow her destiny."

"Yes, she must," said Adam.

"Mmm. Especially if the destiny follows your own, yes?" Miss Maxwell smiled.

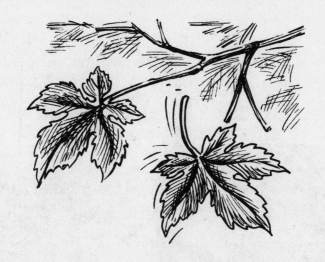

CHAPTER SIXTEEN

Leaving Childhood Behind

Rebecca had barely told Adam Ladd good-bye when Mr. and Mrs. Cobb came to her side.

"Where—where is Aunt Jane?" she cried.

"I'm sorry, lovey, but we've got bad news."

"Is Aunt Miranda worse? She is! I can see it by your looks." Rebecca's color faded.

"She had a second stroke yesterday morning jest when she was helpin' Jane lay out her things to come here today. Jane said you wasn't to know anything about it till graduation was all over."

"I will go right home with you, Aunt Sarah. Poor Aunt Miranda! And I've been so happy all day, except that I missed Mother and Aunt Jane."

"There ain't no harm in bein' happy, lovey. That's what Jane wanted you to be."

"I'll pack your trunk for you, Becky," said Emma Jane. She had come toward them and heard the sad news.

They moved into one of the quiet side pews, where Hannah and Will and John joined them. Classmates called out to Rebecca: "Don't be late for the picnic lunch!" and "Come early to the class party tonight!" But all the excitement became a blur to her. Nothing seemed real.

Aunt Miranda's mind was perfectly clear when Rebecca got to the brick house. She could not move, however. Her pale, sharp face, framed in its nightcap, looked so tired on the pillow. Her body was so very still under the blanket.

"Let me look at you," said the old aunt in her cracked, weak voice. "I hope you won't neglect things in the kitchen because I ain't there. Do you still clean out the coffeepot and turn it upside down on the windowsill?"

"Yes, Aunt Miranda."

"It's always 'yes' with you, and 'yes' with Jane," groaned Miranda. "But I lay here knowin' there's things done the way I don't like 'em."

Rebecca sat down by the bedside and timidly touched her aunt's hand. Her heart swelled with tender pity at the thin face and closed eyes.

"You're not to worry about anything. Here I am all grown up and graduated. Look at me, big and strong and young, all ready to go into the world and show what you and Aunt Jane have done for me. I've had two good positions offered to me already. If you want me near, I'll take the Edgewood school. That way I can be here nights and Sundays to help. When you get better, then I'll go to Augusta. That's a hundred dollars more, with music lessons and other things beside."

"You listen to me," said Miranda in a shaky voice. "Take the best place, regardless of my sickness. I'd like to live long enough to know you'd paid off that mortgage, but I guess I won't."

Here the old woman stopped. This was the most she had talked in weeks. Rebecca went out of the room, to cry by herself.

The days went on, and Miranda grew stronger. Before long she could be moved into a chair by the window. Little by little, hope stole back into Rebecca's young heart. She began to get her clothes ready to go to Augusta.

At length the day dawned when her trunk was packed. Then, when all was ready, a telegram came from Hannah:

COME AT ONCE.
MOTHER HAS HAD A BAD ACCIDENT.

In less than an hour, Rebecca was on her way to Sunnybrook Farm instead of Augusta. There she found that her mother's right knee was broken and her back was strained from a fall. She was in no danger, but she had to stay in bed.

Rebecca wrote the news to her aunts. After they read the letter, Miranda gathered the strength to talk.

"There's things I want to go over with you, Jane. Don't tell Rebecca. I've willed her the brick house. But now, mind you, I *do* plan to take my time 'bout dyin'. And I don't want to be thanked, neither. I s'pose she'll use the front stairs as instead of the back stairs… but, well, maybe when I've been dead a few years I won't let that bother me. She'll want you to stay and have your home here as long as you live. But anyway, I've wrote it down that way."

Jane knit silently as she looked at the poor, sad figure lying weakly on the pillows. She only stopped knitting from time to time to wipe the tears from her own eyes.

Two months went by for Rebecca at Sunnybrook Farm. It was two months of steady, tiring work and weary nights of watching by her mother's bedside.

Rebecca thought of those splendid visions she had during graduation! How fleeting they were. Now her life was filled with dull daily duty. Then one day she received a letter from the school in Augusta. The music position had been filled. Her spirit sagged. Her heart ached. She felt like it was beating against the door of a cage. She longed for the freedom of the big world outside.

But there were moments of joy during those gray days of daily living. As she stirred a cake, or kneaded bread dough, her imagination still wandered. And as she listened to the kitchen fire crackling, and the teakettle whistling, she found herself singing. Her heart had not lost its wings.

The bare little farmhouse *was* dreary, but the children's love for her was comforting. And mother and daughter began to know each other in a new way—as two grown women.

One mellow October morning, Rebecca came into her mother's room with her arms full of autumn leaves. It was a marvelous morning. The air was fragrant with ripening fruit. There was a funny little bird on a tree outside the door nearly bursting his throat with joy of living. He had forgotten that summer was over, and winter was coming. Aurelia heard the bird and looked at her tall, splendid daughter.

Then suddenly she covered her eyes and cried, "I can't bear it! Here I lie chained to this bed, keeping you from everything you want to do. It's all wasted! All my saving and doing without. All your hard study. All Mirandy's money goin' for school and clothes. Everything that we thought was going to be the making of you!"

"Mother, Mother, don't talk so, don't think so!" exclaimed Rebecca. "Why, Mother, I'm only a little past seventeen! The old maple by the well that's a hundred years old had new leaves this summer—so there must be hope for me!"

"I only hope you won't have to wait too long for your leaves, Rebecca," she said. "Your life looks very hard and rough to me. Your Aunt Miranda is a cripple at the brick house. You're taking care of me here at the farm. You've had to work hand and foot, nursing first your aunt and then me."

"I suppose there *ought* to be fears in my heart," Rebecca said. She walked to the window and looked out at the trees. "But there aren't. Something stronger sweeps them out— something like a wind. Oh, Mother! There is Hannah's husband, Will, driving up the lane. He ought to have a letter from the brick house."

CHAPTER SEVENTEEN

"Good-bye, Sunnybrook"

Will Melville drove up to the window. He tossed a letter into Rebecca's lap, then went off to the barn on an errand.

Rebecca opened the envelope. In one flash of an eye she read the whole brief page.

Your Aunt Miranda passed away an hour ago. Come at once, if your mother is out of danger. I shall not have the funeral till you are here. She died very suddenly and without any pain.

Oh, Rebecca! I long for you so!

—Aunt Jane

Rebecca burst into a passion of tears. "Poor, poor Aunt Miranda! She is gone without ever really being happy in life. And I couldn't say good-bye to her! Poor lonely Aunt Jane! What can I do, Mother? I feel torn in two, between you and the brick house."

"You must go this very instant," said Aurelia, raising herself from her pillows. "Your aunts have done everything in the world for you. It is your turn to pay back some of their kindness and show your gratitude. Jenny can take care of the house somehow, if Hannah will come over once a day.

"Oh, how I wish I could go to my sister's funeral. I'd like to tell her that I've forgotten and forgiven all she said when I was married. Her acts were softer than her words.

"I remember so well when we were little girls together. She took such pride in curling my hair. Another time, when we were grown up, she let me wear her best blue muslin dress. It was when Lorenzo—before he was your father!—had asked me to lead the grand march with him at the Christmas dance. And I found out afterward that Miranda thought he would ask her! And still, she lent me her dress."

There was only an hour to pack. Will Melville would drive Rebecca to Temperance. A neighbor lady would sleep at the farm in case Mrs. Randall needed any help in the night.

Rebecca flew down over the hill to get a last pail of spring water. As she lifted the bucket from the crystal brook, she looked out over the glowing beauty of the autumn landscape. She saw a group of men looking though some instruments of some kind. They were writing in notebooks, and had strung lines of rope between posts in the ground.

The lines crossed Sunnybrook at her favorite spot where the pond lay clear and still. Yellow leaves sat on its quiet surface. Its sand was sparkling in the sun. Rebecca knew at once what the men were doing. They were surveying land for the new railway.

She caught her breath.

The time has come! she thought. *I am saying good-bye to Sunnybrook. The gates that almost swung together that last day in Wareham will close forever, now. Good-bye, dear brook and hills and meadows. You are going to see life, too. We must be always hopeful that the best is yet to be.*

Will had seen the surveyors, too. At the post office, he heard how much Mrs. Randall was sure to get for her land. He was very pleased! His land was next to hers, and it would be more valuable, now, also. In the buggy, he felt like whistling all the way to Temperance. But Rebecca's own sad face kept him quiet.

"Cheer up, Becky!" he said, as he left her at the station. "Your mother will be fine soon. And the next thing you know, your family will be moving to some nice little house close to wherever you work." Then he drove away to tell Hannah the good news.

Adam Ladd was waiting at the train station. He came up to Rebecca as she entered the door.

"I know you are sad this morning," he said, taking her hand.

She opened her heart and told him of her grief. He gave her his sympathy and asked if he might come soon to the brick house to see her.

He helped her on the train to Maplewood, and they said their good-byes. Adam thought that Rebecca was, in her sad dignity, more beautiful than he had ever seen her. She was a beautiful person—and a beautiful woman.

He turned from the little country station to walk in the woods until his own train would be leaving. There he threw himself under a tree to think and dream. He had brought a new copy of *The Arabian Nights* for Rebecca. He wanted to replace her well-worn old one. But he had forgotten to give it to her—after meeting at such a sad time.

He turned the pages slowly, and came to the story of "Aladdin and the Wonderful Lamp." The old tale held him spellbound, just as it had in the days when he first read it as a boy. But there was one part he found himself reading over and over. This was the part where Aladdin is filled with happiness because the princess admits that she loves him and wishes to marry him.

CHAPTER EIGHTEEN

Aunt Miranda's Apology

Rebecca got off the train at Maplewood and hurried to the stagecoach to Riverboro. She was overjoyed to see Uncle Jerry Cobb standing there next to the horses.

"My drivin' days are over," he explained, "but I came for you. So here I am, jest as I was more'n six year ago. Will ya sit up in front with me?" A warm smile spread across the old man's face.

Rebecca flung herself on Mr. Cobb's dusty shoulder, crying like a child.

"Oh, Uncle Jerry!" she sobbed. "It's all so long ago, and so much has happened. And so much is *going* to happen that I'm fairly frightened."

"There, there, lovey," the old man whispered. "We'll talk things over as we go along the road. Maybe things won't look so bad."

Every mile of the way was familiar. And all the time, Rebecca was thinking back to the day, so long ago, when she sat on the box seat for the first time. Her legs had dangled in the air, too short to reach the footboard. She could see the pink parasol, and feel the stiffness of the tan dress. The two friends drove along mostly in silence. But it was a sweet, comforting silence to both of them.

In Riverboro, she saw a white cloth fluttering from the Perkins' attic window. It was Emma Jane's loving "hello" to warm her heart until they could meet. Black scarves hung over the blinds of the brick house. The brass knocker was covered with a black cloth.

"Stop, Uncle Jerry! Don't turn in at the side. Let me run up the path by myself."

The door of the brick house opened just as Rebecca closed the gate behind her. Aunt Jane came down the stone steps, frail and white. Rebecca held out her arms. Then, warmth and strength and life flowed from the young lady into the older woman.

"Rebecca," she said, raising her head, "before you go in to look at her, do you feel any bitterness over anything she ever said to you?"

Rebecca's eyes blazed. She said in a choking voice, "Oh, Aunt Jane! I am going in with a heart full of gratitude!"

"She was a good woman, Rebecca. She had a quick temper and a sharp tongue, but she wanted to do right. And she did it as near as she could. She never said so, but I'm sure she was sorry for every hard word she spoke to you. She didn't take her words back in life. But she acted so that you'd know her feelings when she was gone."

"I told her before I left that she really had been the making of me," sobbed Rebecca.

"God made you in the first place. And I'd say you've done a lot yourself to help Him along," said Aunt Jane. "But she gave you the means to do it and that ain't to be looked down on. And she did give up some of her own luxuries to do it. Now let me tell you something, Rebecca. Your Aunt Mirandy has left all this to you in her will. The brick house and buildings. All the furniture. And the land all round the house."

Rebecca put her hand to her heart. After a moment's silence she said, "Let me go in alone. I want to talk to her. I want to thank her. I feel as if I could make her hear and feel and understand."

Jane went back into the kitchen. Even death does not stop daily duties. The table still must be laid, the dishes washed, and the beds made, by somebody.

Ten minutes later, Rebecca came outside from the parlor looking white and tired, but calm. She sat in the quiet doorway. Here she was shaded from the little Riverboro world by the overhanging elms. A wide sense of thankfulness and peace came over her as she looked at the autumn landscape. She listened to the rumble of a wagon on the bridge. She heard the call of the river as it dashed to the sea. She put up her hand softly and touched first the shining brass knocker and then the red bricks, glowing in the October sun.

It was home—her roof, her garden, her green acres, her dear trees. It was shelter for the little family at Sunnybrook. Her mother and Aunt Jane would once more be together. Her mother would be with old friends from her girlhood. The children would have teachers and playmates.

And she? Her own future was still folded and closed from view. It was folded and hidden in beautiful mists. She leaned her head against the sun-warmed door. She closed her eyes and whispered, just as if she had been a child saying her prayers:

"God bless Aunt Miranda. God bless the brick house that was. God bless the brick house that is to be!"

THE END

KATE DOUGLAS WIGGIN

Kate Douglas Smith was born in Philadelphia in 1856. Her father died when she was young, and her family moved to Maine. There, her mother remarried and they settled in the small town of Hollis. Much like Rebecca Randall, Kate received her education through home study, district school, a female seminary, and an academy. This was a lot of education for a girl of her times!

Kate began teaching kindergarten in 1877 and soon started Silver Street Kindergarten in San Francisco, the first kindergarten in California. She married Bradley Wiggin in 1881. As a married woman, she was not allowed to teach, but she still loved children. Her first books, including *The Birds' Christmas Carol*, were written to raise money for the Kindergarten.

When Kate's first husband died suddenly in 1889, she began writing more. In 1895 she married George Christopher Riggs, who strongly supported her writing. *Rebecca of Sunnybrook Farm*, Kate's most famous book, was written in 1903.

She died in Harrow, England, August 24, 1923, while attending a writing conference.